Brady Brady
and the Big Mistake

Written by Mary Shaw

Illustrated by Chuck Temple

PUBLISHED BY
BRADY BRADY INC

Text copyright © 2001 by Mary Shaw
Illustrations copyright © 2001 by Chuck Temple
Visit **www.bradybrady.com** for more Brady Brady information

Published in Canada in 2004 by

Brady Brady Inc.
P.O. Box 367
Waterloo, Ontario
Canada
N2J 4A4

Canadian Cataloguing in Publication Data

ISBN 0-9735557-4-2

Brady's friends are coming to his house to skate, and he
wants it to be the perfect day. To make it extra special, he decides to
borrow his father's most cherished hockey souvenir - a puck signed by
Bobby Orr - even though he's not allowed to play with it.

Printed and bound in Canada

Keep adding to your Brady Brady book collection. Make sure you read:

• **Brady Brady and the Great Rink** • **Brady Brady and the Runaway Goalie**
• **Brady Brady and the Twirlin' Torpedo** • **Brady Brady and the Singing Tree**
• **Brady Brady and the Big Mistake** • **Brady Brady and the Great Exchange**
• **Brady Brady and the Most Important Game** • **Brady Brady and the MVP**

For my parents, Peter and Sandra Cote.
Thank you for all you have done for me
Mary Shaw

For my good friends:
Vic, Mark, Bill, Fred and Alex
Chuck Temple

It was the perfect afternoon for a game of shinny — and the perfect place was Brady's backyard rink.

Brady shoveled off the ice rink and put out the nets.
He wanted everything to be just right for his friends.

That's when the idea hit him.

Brady flung his boots and mitts off at the back door, raced into the house and down the hall, straight to the room with the closed door. This was his dad's office. It was filled with stacks upon stacks of old hockey magazines, dusty trophies, hockey cards, and autographed pictures and programs.

But there was something that was more important than everything else.

It lay in a gold velvet case, smack in the middle of the desk. It was his father's special, signed puck. *This* puck had once been stick-handled and blasted into the net by his dad's idol . . . Number 4 . . . Bobby Orr!

Brady had been allowed to hold it lots of times, but only when his dad was there. This was different, but Brady told himself that his dad wouldn't mind. After all, pucks were meant to be played with.

Still, his hand trembled a little as he carefully lifted the puck out of its case. It felt warm in his cool fingers. He **had** to show it off to his friends!

Through the window, Brady could see them arriving.
Quickly, he stuffed the special puck in his pocket
and rushed to put his skates on.

"Hey everybody, check this out!" Brady hollered when he reached the yard. He held out the puck and the kids crowded around.

"What are we supposed to check out?" Tes asked with a grin. "It looks like a puck to me."

"Yeah," chuckled Tree. "We've seen a puck before, Brady Brady."

"Not this one, you haven't," said Brady, holding it higher. "This puck was used by Bobby Orr, one of the greatest hockey players ever! It's even signed by him," Brady boasted. "It's my dad's, and he won't mind if we try it out!"

As soon as he said it, Brady felt a butterfly in his stomach.
But then he saw the smiles on his teammates' faces.

He threw the puck onto the ice and tried to skate like Bobby Orr. As fast as he could, he circled the rink, shifting the puck from side to side on the end of his stick. Stopping in a spray of snow, he was thrilled to see how impressed his friends were.

So, the game of shinny began. The Icehogs were **sure** the puck had special powers. Chester said it almost blew a hole right through his glovehand! Tes said her "Twirlin' Torpedo" slapshot sailed faster than ever!

And then . . . Brady got a breakaway.

Racing toward the net, he imagined that he was a famous hockey player carrying the puck up the ice for the big goal of the game. He took aim at the top corner of the net — and fired.

It went flying, over Chester, over the net,
and disappeared into the ***biggest*** snowbank in the whole backyard!

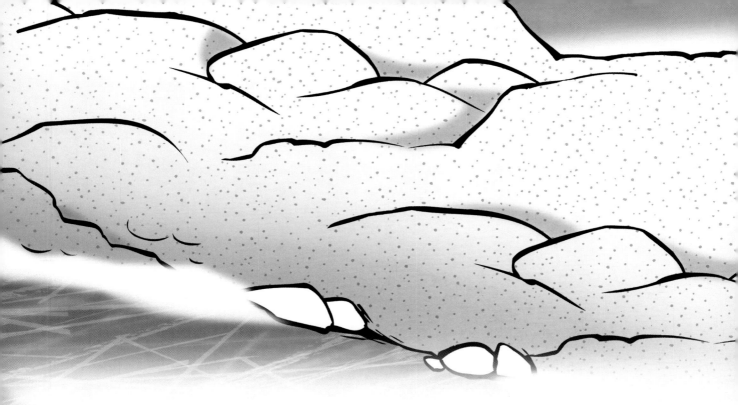

Everything stopped. Everyone fell silent.

Beads of sweat trickled down Brady's face, but they weren't from his breakaway. They were from the thought of his dad's special Bobby Orr puck *lost* in all that snow.

Brady and his teammates scrambled over the smaller snowbanks and into the *huge* pile of snow that had swallowed the puck.

"We'd better hurry up and find it," Brady said. "The street lights are coming on. That means my dad will be home soon."

Snow flew every which way as the Icehogs frantically searched for the missing puck.

One by one, they flopped, exhausted, into the snow.

"*What* am I going to tell my dad???" Brady cried, burying his face in his hands.

"Maybe you could tell him Bobby Orr called and asked for his puck back," Tree suggested, trying to be helpful.

"You could tell him that you took it to a sports store to get the nicks and scrapes repaired," offered Chester.

Brady looked up at the pile of snow.
How could he have made such a big mistake???

His father had taken special care of that puck because it meant so much to him. Brady hadn't thought about how his dad might feel knowing his prized puck was being whacked around on the ice. He had only thought about how *he* would feel showing it off to his friends.

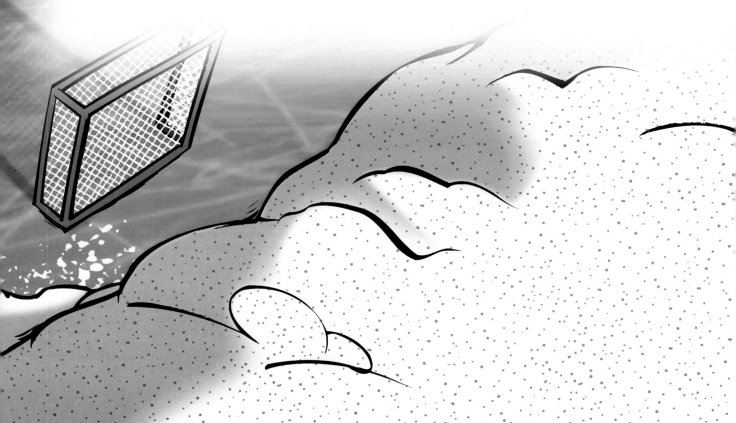

Brady heard the car pull into the driveway. He couldn't move. His friends felt badly for him, wondering what he was going to tell his dad.

Brady's dad walked into the backyard.

"Hi kids! Having fun?" he asked. But nobody answered. They couldn't even look at him.

Then in the silence, a small voice spoke up.

"I need to tell you something, Dad," Brady mumbled, "and you're not going to like it." Brady's eyes met his father's. "You know your autographed puck that I'm just suppose to *look* at? Well, I did more than *look* at it. I picked it up."

Brady's dad grinned knowingly and nodded. "I understand, Brady Brady. It's hard not to want to pick it up. It's pretty special."

Brady interrupted. "I didn't just pick it up, though, Dad. I told the kids that we could play with it . . . I took a wrist shot . . ." Brady gulped. ". . . a wrist shot right into that *huge* snowbank!"

Brady and his friends all pointed at the sinister heap.

His dad's smile disappeared, and his eyes blinked in disbelief. At that moment, Brady was afraid he had broken his father's trust **and** his heart.

"I'm really, really sorry. Even if it takes me until spring, I won't stop looking for that puck," Brady said.

Brady's dad squeezed his shoulder and looked at him.

"To be honest, I am disappointed that you took the puck without my permission. But believe it or not, Brady Brady, your telling me the truth about what happened means more to me than any puck — even that one. And do you know what else?" he added. "You won't have to look for it until spring. I'll help you now." Brady's dad gave him a wink.

"Why don't we start by looking in Hatrick's doghouse!"